Clarence the crocodile

by
Griselda Gifford

Illustrated by
Frances Thatcher

Nelson

Thomas Nelson and Sons Ltd
Nelson House   Mayfield Road
Walton-on-Thames   Surrey
KT12 5PL   UK

51 York Place
Edinburgh
EH1 3JD   UK

Thomas Nelson (Hong Kong) Ltd
Toppan Building 10/F
22A Westlands Road
Quarry Bay   Hong Kong

Thomas Nelson Australia
102 Dodds Street
South Melbourne
Victoria 3205   Australia

Nelson Canada
1120 Birchmount Road
Scarborough Ontario
M1K 5G4   Canada

© Macmillan Education Ltd 1987
This edition © Thomas Nelson & Sons Ltd 1992
Editorial Consultant: Donna Bailey
Written by Griselda Gifford
Illusrated by Frances Thatcher

First published by Macmillan Education Ltd 1987
ISBN 0-333-41892-1

This edition published by Thomas Nelson and Sons Ltd 1992

ISBN 0-17-422530-X
NPN 9 8 7 6 5 4 3 2

Printed in Hong Kong

Chapter 1: Clarence is bored

Clarence was a crocodile.
He lived by the river with his father and
his mother and his six sisters.
His father and mother and his six sisters
were all green, as green as grass, but
Clarence was white, as white as snow.

Clarence tried to look green like
the other crocodiles.
He rolled in the river mud, but that
only made him a dirty white and
made his mother cross.
It didn't make him green and Clarence so wanted
to be green like the other crocodiles.

4

"Poor Clarence," said his mother.
She tried to hide him from his aunts and uncles.
She sent him away when they came to visit.
"Wash in the river," she would say and
when he came back from the river,
his aunts and uncles had always gone.
Clarence was very sad.
He cried big crocodile tears.
"Nobody likes white crocodiles,"
he said to himself.

Clarence knew that his mother was ashamed of him.

He heard his mother and father talking.

"There has never been a white crocodile in our family," they said.

Clarence wished and wished he was green.

He also wished he did not have to
sit still so much.

"Sit still in a row and pretend to be logs,"
his father said to them all.

The crocodiles lay in a row by the river.
Sometimes they opened their mouths wide and
showed all their big teeth, but most of the time
they just lay still by the river and
pretended to be logs.

"Why must I sit still?" asked Clarence.

"Because all crocodiles do," said his mother.

"Why?" he asked again. "I'm bored with sitting still. And why am I white?"

"You just are," said his mother sadly. "Perhaps you cannot sit still because you are white."

Clarence opened his mouth wide and yawned.

"I'm bored," he said again to himself.

Clarence's father and mother went to sleep.
Clarence wriggled over to his six sisters and
tickled them with the tip of his long tail.

"Mum! Clarence is tickling us!" they all shouted.

"Be quiet at once Clarence!" said his father.
"Sit still or you will not have any mud-playtime."

Clarence loved mud-playtime.
The little crocodiles went deep down
into the lovely river mud.
So he sat still for one minute.
But he was still very bored.
   Then he had an idea.
He knew what he would do.
He would run away!
He waited until his mother and father and
his six sisters were asleep again, then
he wriggled very, very quietly into
the deep green jungle.
Nobody saw him run away.

Chapter 2: Clarence runs away

At first Clarence found it very exciting to run away.
Creepers hung down over the paths.
Beautiful flowers grew on the bushes and
big butterflies flew past.
Blue and red and yellow parrots flew above him.
Huge insects hummed and buzzed around him.
Clarence had never been on his own before.
It was a big adventure. He was very happy.

Then he began to feel lonely.
A long snake wriggled over the path.
Clarence said "Hello!" but the snake only hissed.
   A big striped tiger ran up.
Clarence was scared.
   "Hello," he said, but the tiger just looked at him.
Then it ran away into the jungle.

A family of monkeys came through
the bushes.
Clarence was very scared.
"Hello. I'm Clarence," he said
in a small voice.
The monkeys did not even look at him.
They just went on through the jungle.
Suddenly there was a great roar and
a lion came slowly towards him.
It was very, very big and it looked hungry.
Clarence was glad he had a hard scaly skin.
The lion would get hiccups if he ate Clarence!

Clarence opened his mouth to show that
he had a lot of sharp teeth and said in
a small squeaky voice, "Hello. I'm Clarence."

The lion looked at Clarence and then
walked past, waving his tail in the air.
He came so close that he almost walked
on Clarence!

Clarence was sad.
None of the animals wanted to talk to him.
He felt lonely and he felt hungry and
he felt hot.
He must find the river again.

Chapter 3: Clarence makes some new friends

Clarence walked on and on.
He got hotter and hotter and his legs were tired.
Then at last he saw the river.
Clarence sank happily into the cool dark mud.
Then he swam out to find a fish to eat.
Snap! Clarence had caught a large fish.
It filled his tummy so much that he felt quite full.

Clarence was not hungry any more, but
he still had an empty feeling inside.
What was it? He thought hard.
He was not hot now and he was not hungry,
but he was still lonely. He must find a friend.
     Clarence set off and swam down the river.
He swam round the first bend in the river,
then he swam round the next bend,
and the next.
But he was still all alone.

Then round the next bend, Clarence
suddenly saw a big family of crocodiles.
They were swimming down the river
in front of him.
Clarence could not believe his eyes, for
all the crocodiles were white, white all over,
just like him!

"Hello!" he shouted and the crocodile family
all swam up to him.
He was not alone any more.

"I'm Clarence," he said.

The crocodiles all smiled at him, showing their big white teeth.

There was a mother and a father and seven children.

"You are white, like me!" Clarence said, smiling back at the crocodiles.

"All crocodiles are white," said the father.

"Well, nearly all," said the mother.

"It's the right colour," said the father.

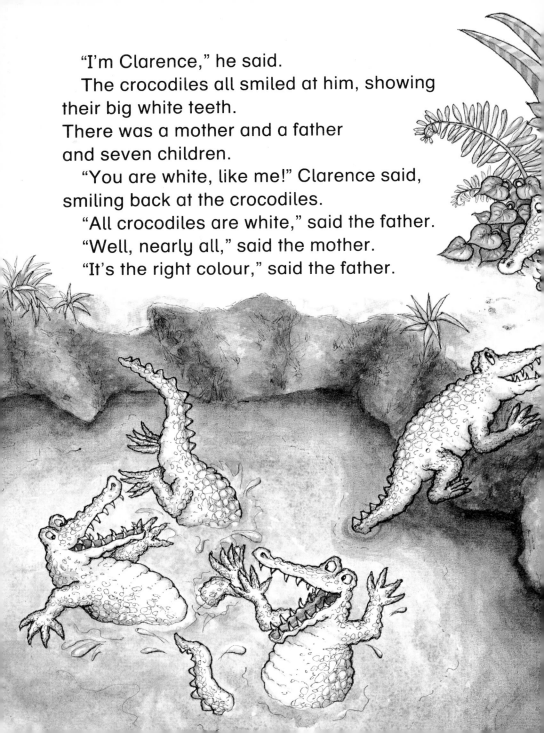

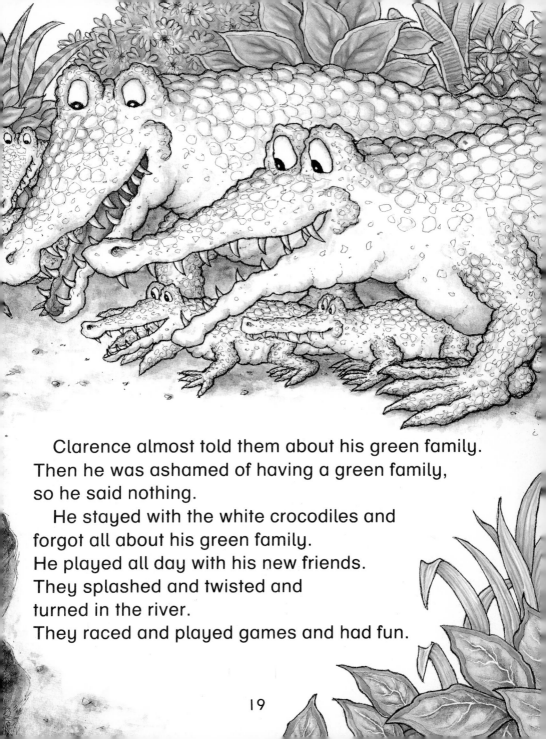

Clarence almost told them about his green family.
Then he was ashamed of having a green family,
so he said nothing.

He stayed with the white crocodiles and
forgot all about his green family.
He played all day with his new friends.
They splashed and twisted and
turned in the river.
They raced and played games and had fun.

19

Chapter 4: Clarence helps Emily

Later that day, Clarence's new mother
called the children.

"Time to sit still," she said and
gave Clarence a push with her nose.
Her family sat on the bank with their big mouths open.

"Oh, no. Not here too!" Clarence thought.
He did not want to sit still.
He would be bored again.
Why did all crocodiles have to sit still?

Clarence sat on the bank, feeling bored.
Then he heard a crying sound from the mud below.
He saw a crocodile nose sticking out of the mud.

"Who is that crying?" he asked.

"It's only Emily. She is our sister,"
said the white crocodiles. "She is always crying."

"She is green," one of them said. "That's
why she cries."

"We've never had a green crocodile in
our family before," said the mother crossly.

Emily lifted her head out of the mud.
She sobbed even louder.

"But she is so unhappy," said Clarence.

"Oh, leave her alone," said the white
crocodile family. "She will not sit still like us.
Green crocodiles are stupid, you know," they said.

Clarence was sad about Emily.
He slid down the bank and into the mud.
   "You will miss the fish for tea,"
called the others.
"Fancy liking green crocodiles," they said.
   Clarence took no notice of them.
He went up to Emily and touched her nose.
   "Nobody likes me because I'm green," she cried.

Clarence was sorry for Emily.

"My family are all green," he said. "And they said I could not sit still because I was white."

"That is what they say to me," sniffed Emily. "You cannot sit still because you are green, they say."

"Let's look for a mud-playtime place of our own," said Clarence.

"Oh yes," said Emily. "Let's do that!"

So Clarence and Emily went away and
found a nice bit of thick deep mud where
they played and splashed all day long.
Soon they were both so dirty that
they were both black.
You could not see which crocodile was white
and which crocodile was green.
They caught fish and ate them for dinner
and were happy all day long.

They twisted and turned in the water.
They wriggled and wriggled on the bank and
never sat still.
They had great fun.

"Green crocodiles are not stupid," said Emily.

"And I like being white now," said Clarence.

"I am not lonely now I have met you."

"Neither am I," said Emily.

Chapter 5: The family

When Clarence and Emily grew up, they married.
They had a family.
Emily laid three large eggs.
Then one day the eggs began to hatch.
The first little crocodile came out of his egg.
He was white.
The second baby crocodile came out of his egg.
He was green.
Clarence and Emily were very excited.
What colour would the third baby be?

Clarence thought it would be green, like Emily.
Emily hoped it would be white, like Clarence.
They waited for the baby to come out of the egg.
Slowly the baby wriggled out.
It was not green. It was not white.
It was striped!
It had lovely green and white stripes on
its small wriggly body.

Clarence and Emily named the first baby
Boko and the second baby Zoko.
They called the third baby who had
such lovely stripes Toto.
   Boko and Zoko and Toto played together
all day long.
They twisted and turned in the river water.
They were happy.
Sometimes they rolled in the mud.
Emily and Clarence just smiled
big crocodile smiles and never told them
not to wriggle, or made them sit still.

One day Toto was crying.

"Boko and Zoko laugh at me because I am striped," she said.

Clarence looked at Emily.
They both smiled wide crocodile smiles.

"It is only because you are different," Clarence said.

"Tell them that stripes are special," said Emily.

They gave Toto a large fish to eat.

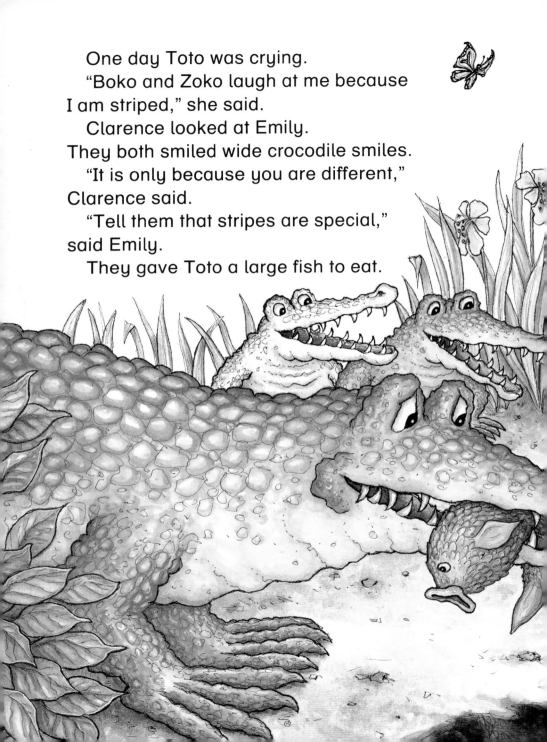

"Stripes are special," Toto mumbled as
she chewed her fish.
Then she sat with her mouth open, smiling
and showing all her teeth.
She was happy.
   "Stripes are special," she told Boko and Zoko.
They looked at her.

"I am green and white," Toto said, "because part of me is like my mother and part of me is like my father."

"We will not laugh at you any more," said Boko and Zoko.

Clarence saw them all playing happily together.

"If all crocodiles were striped, none of them would be lonely," he said.

Emily looked up out of the mud.

"Glug," she said, which of course meant "Yes."